I0445782

MARIE-HÉLÈNE LEBEAULT

AUTHOR OF THE EVERS SERIES

A SUMMER

OF

DISCOVERY

DEFENDERS OF THE REALM - NOVELLA ONE

First published by Beaches and Trails Publishing 2023
Copyright © 2023 by Marie-Hélène Lebeault

All rights reserved.
No part of this publication may be reproduced, stored or transmitted in any form or by
any means, electronic, mechanical, photocopying, recording, scanning, or otherwise
without written permission from the publisher. It is illegal to copy this book, post it to a
website, or distribute it by any other means without permission.
This is a work of fiction.

First edition

Editing by Rachael Lammie
Proofreading by Alli Wait
Cover by GetCovers

About the Author

Marie-Helene Lebeault lives in Quebec, Canada and is the mother of two young adults. A retired teacher, she now spends her days writing, translating academic manuals, and lending her voice to corporate training videos. She enjoys reading, hiking, and going to the beach. She is also an avid rollercoaster fiend and is on a mission to visit all the Six Flags amusement parks with her daughter. Every year, she travels for three weeks on a solo adventure to a new part of the world.

Follow on Social Media, she'd love to hear from you!

Website Email Newsletter

facebook.com/mhlebeaultauthor
x.com/mhlebeault
instagram.com/mhlebeault
amazon.com/author/mhlebeault
bookbub.com/authors/marie-helene-lebeault
goodreads.com/mhlebeault
linkedin.com/in/mhlebeault
tiktok.com/@mhlebeaultauthor
youtube.com/@mhlebeault

ALSO BY THE AUTHOR

The Chronicles of the Starborne Cadets

Stars Beyond Realms

Shadows of Orion

Echoes of the Void

The Nebula's Heart

The Starborne Paradox

Defenders of the Realm

A Journey to Power

The Quest for the Emerald Rattleback

A Summer of Discovery

The Quest for the Sacred Tree

A Summer of Opposites

The Quest for the Phantom Feather

A Summer of Courage

The Quest for the Kraken's Ink

A Summer of Destiny

The Quest for the Cursed Mirrors

The Evers Series

The Ancestors' Key

The Academy

The Time Walker

The World Jumper

Blood Magick Trilogy

The Blood Mage

Blood Magick

Blood Legacy

Standalones

Clarity Castle

What Happens Next?

Ghost Stories

Holiday Shifters

Echoes of Tomorrow

Utopia

Picture Books

Fairy Grandmother: Millie Goes to Antarctica

Fairy Grandmother: Millie Goes to the North Pole

Fairy Grandmother: Millie Goes to China

Fairy Grandmother: Millie Goes to Africa

(Also available in French, Spanish, German, and Italian)

CHAPTER
ONE

After an eventful year, the students had gone home for the summer; the professors had arranged how they would take their vacations, and all was peaceful at the Institute of Eldavon once again. A handful of students would stay for the summer, and the responsibility to keep them busy fell to the two headmasters, Twila and Valiant.

"We need to give them something besides responsibilities and work," Twila said, her arm through Valiant's as they took their nightly 'date walk' around the Institute campus.

Valiant nodded, considering the conundrum. With the current political tension between Eldavon and Odentia, it would do the students some good to have something to take their minds off their troubles.

They'd walked this path so many times over the last few decades since they were named headmasters that Twila could describe every step of the way with her eyes closed—a feat she had proved half a dozen times or so over the years.

"We could always have another play or communal art project," Valiant replied. His back was giving him some trouble lately, meaning they walked a little slower than they once had, but the night was so warm and lovely that he didn't want to miss it.

"We could," Twila agreed. "I'm afraid it won't offer as much mental stimulation as we could want... oh, look."

She nodded up the hill to the bench swing between two trees. Light stones dangled through the branches, illuminating the young woman who sat on the bench. Herja, her inky-black hair having grown just long enough to pull back, swung as she read. A giggle reached the two headmasters, and Twila arched a brow.

"I don't think I've heard Herja giggle before," she whispered.

"We should give her some space," Valiant started, but his wife, and dragon-match, had already started up the hill.

He rolled his black eyes but smiled as he followed her. Herja didn't notice them until they were at the bench, and then she gave a big jerk and snapped her book shut. She slid it beneath the book bag she had with her. Her cheeks turned brilliantly red as she jumped to her feet.

"Headmasters. I didn't expect to see you here," she squeaked.

Valiant lifted an eyebrow. It wasn't like Herja to get flustered. What was she reading that she would be so embarrassed? "We were just out walking... what are you reading?"

"Nothing," Herja said quickly.

Twila laughed. "Oh, you're just making yourself look guilty, Herja. Now let's see. Is it something wildly inappropriate?"

"Twila," Valiant chided, though he was just as curious. The library was full of books for all ages, and Herja was just the type of child to read things that weren't written for her age group.

"I'm only reading a book," Herja protested. "It was in the second-year section."

Twila poked at the book bag. "Pleeeease?"

Herja rolled her eyes. "Oh, fine! If you're going to be weird about it."

"Twila is always weird," Valiant replied mildly. "It's her most treasured personality trait."

Twila laughed in response, as Valiant knew she would. She took the book offered by Herja and hummed. "Oh, I see. You're getting into

2

romances now—no, no," she quickly added as Herja's blush deepened. "That's not a bad thing, Herja. Studying is all well and good, but relaxation is just as important. And this one was my favorite when I was your age... still is, in fact. There's something about fake dating that's just top shelf."

Herja took the book back, smiling a little now.

"Ah, romance." Valiant put his arm around Twila's waist. "Are you enjoying it?"

"Umm... yes, more than I thought I would," Herja admitted. She fidgeted on the spot before she settled on the bench. "I'm only reading a romance novel because I wanted to know what it was like... since we're getting our fated mates next year. I'm just... I'm worried I won't do it right, and my mate will hate me."

Valiant sat on the other end of the bench, rubbing his lower back. Twila took a seat between them, and they shared a glance; at fifteen years old, the idea of fated mates was both thrilling and terrifying.

"It's normal for you to be worried about it," Twila told Herja comfortingly. "It's a difficult thing, especially when whom you end up matched with is beyond your control. But the bond is strong enough to overcome all obstacles."

Herja kicked her feet into the ground. "But that's just what I'm afraid of. What if they hate me so much that there is no bond? I know I'm not the easiest person to like...."

"It's not a one-way street, you know. If they are upset with being matched with you, learn how to be patient and let them work through their feelings," Valiant said. "You know, Twila and I didn't like each other when we were matched together."

"Really?" Herja asked, the doubt clear on her face.

"Indeed."

"But you're both so... perfect for each other," Herja protested.

Twila nodded once. "And we have put in a lot of effort to get our relationship to this point. You see, we didn't like each other. Both of us wanted to be mated to someone else. I was in love—or at least, infatuated—with a witch named Howard."

"And I was in love with a human named Giselle."

"But dragons and witches are always mated to each other," Herja said. "Why would you think a human could be your match?"

Valiant shook his head. "If you had a thousand dragons, nine hundred and ninety-nine would be matched with a witch. But there are those rare cases where a dragon matches with another dragon or a witch matches with another witch, or either one could match with a human."

"But fated mates are chosen mates for a reason," Twila continued. "And even though we both had someone else we wanted to be with, the stars had another idea for us."

TWILA PAUSED as she glanced over at Valiant. As memories of that first summer came flooding back, Valiant couldn't help but grin back. Oh, they must have caused so much worry for their own headmasters... "It was a summer to remember, that last one we spent here at the Institute before we graduated."

"We hadn't just been fighting our bond," Twila said. "We'd been fighting over everything. It didn't matter what it was; it didn't even matter if we agreed. We found some way to end up arguing about it. I thought if we proved how incompatible we were, somehow, we could break the bond."

Herja's silver eyes widened. "Can that happen?"

"Yes, of course," Valiant told her. "If a pair really is miserable together, there are ways to break the match. It's not as easy as a divorce and will have lasting repercussions... but as we said, there is a choice in the relationship."

Twila nodded. "It's not right to force two people together if they really, truly don't wish to be together. Especially if there is anything like abuse happening in the relationship, but those are rare, too, even more rare than a witch or dragon being matched with a human."

Herja considered this for a moment, and Valiant took Twila's hand, squeezing lightly. It was best to let the girl process this, after all. It wasn't something that was often discussed. Still, such things did happen. Valiant considered whether they ought to put something in the curriculum... the bond between a mated pair was so strong that there were only a few cases where it would be better to be separate than together.

All the same, they probably ought to have some discussion with the children about the signs of abuse and what resources there were available to both parties in such circumstances.

"If you could have broken the fated bond between the two of you, and you were constantly fighting, why didn't you break it?" Herja asked, her brow furrowed.

Valiant hummed and nodded at Twila to speak first.

She sighed. "I thought about it, of course. I think some part of me hoped we could somehow make it work. I wanted my match. I'd wanted it so badly but had managed to blind myself."

"I, for one, figured we could be just as happy if we remained mated but never spent time with each other," Valiant said. "It's not a marriage, after all. We didn't have to spend the rest of our lives together. And I suppose there was also a part of me that knew even then, the stars knew us better than we knew ourselves...."

CHAPTER

TWO

"We were arguing again," Twila said with a small laugh. "We were always arguing over petty this. This time it was who had left a mess in the common room of our dorm."

Twila grabbed the book that she'd been seeing Valiant reading all the time and threw it onto the table, then plopped into the overstuffed chair herself. "You need to learn how to pick up after yourself," she snapped, glaring at where the witch messed with the fire.

Valiant turned. "Hey! That's my chair."

"Your chair?"

"I left my book on it to save my spot."

Twila scoffed as she slung her legs over the armrest. "How was I supposed to know that? You're always leaving everything around all over the place. I'm always having to pick up your shoes and jackets and—"

"You're the one who never cleans up after yourself," Valiant interrupted. He stood and stomped to the table, where he grabbed his book. "Dirty dishes everywhere. I'm surprised we haven't been infested with rats!"

"You know that Institute is spelled to repel vermin... at least of the four-legged kind," Twila replied nastily.

She knew it was a childish argument. All their fights were. She also knew Valiant well enough to know he wasn't the sort of man who would back down from a fight just because it was childish... and she wasn't the sort of woman who'd stop fighting when her opponent was still fighting.

He was smug enough; she didn't want him to think that he'd won the argument.

The other fifth-year students in the common room glanced at each other as they started packing up their things. Twila ignored them. It was better than them trying to intervene like they normally did. She was sick and tired of Valiant and his smarter-than-you attitude.

"Get out of my chair," Valiant said.

"I don't see your name on it. You didn't buy it."

"You are so immature. I don't know what the stars were thinking, forcing me to be mated to the likes of you," he snapped, his hands clenched at his sides.

Twila's hackles rose. Oh, really? He was going to bring that up again. "I suppose you're still pining after your human girlfriend, even though she's engaged to someone else? I never told you to break up with her. So, you can't keep blaming me on that one, Valiant."

"I never said it was your fault. But it *is* your fault that you're an arrogant—"

"I'm arrogant?" Twila jumped to her feet, furious. "Look in the mirror before you start accusing me of being arrogant, you conceited, egotistical—"

Valiant barked out a harsh laugh. "Those mean the same things!"

"I didn't want you as my mate, either," she shouted, her nails digging into her palms. "But you don't see me throwing it in your face constantly! I never wanted you! I would have been better off with anyone else rather than having to deal with your smug face and attitude for the past three years!"

Valiant threw his hands into the air. "No? You don't think I heard about you crying yourself to sleep every night that first year?"

"I didn't cry myself to sleep ever in my life!" Twila's cheeks turned red with embarrassment.

He was right... she had been so devastated that it took her a long time before she stopped sobbing every night. But how could he even know that? She'd kept herself together while she was in the common areas and only cried when she was in her room, alone.

Which of her roommates had betrayed her?

"Well, you don't have to deal with me much longer," Valiant said, his voice rising. "Once we've graduated, I'm never spending another minute with you. You can run off and do whatever dragon plans you have, and I—"

"And you'll go crawling to that human girlfriend of yours?"

Valiant hissed between his teeth. "I'm going to live my life. I'll forget all about you. I'll fall in love again, and I am going to have a fantastic life. Marriage and children. Everything you don't want to have."

Twila could hardly believe what she was hearing. Where did he get off assuming that she didn't want to be married and have children? It was the one thing that she had hoped would come out of this fated mate match.

He was the one who stole all her dreams.

"Once we're graduated," Valiant said again, "we will never have to see each other again."

She was on the verge of screaming out that she hated him when the door to the common room banged open.

Twila jumped, startled out of the fight. Valiant made a choking sound. The two headmasters, Emmerson and Olivia, strode in. Their expressions said they knew exactly what was going on, and Twila shrank into herself. Her fellow students were one thing... the headmasters were another.

"Office," Headmaster Emmerson snapped. His glowing silver eyes, marking him as a dragon, narrowed on Twila. "Now."

"The same for you," Headmaster Olivia said, her tone not so loud but just as firm as she addressed Valiant.

Twila's shoulders grew increasingly hunched as she followed behind the two headmasters. The argument played through her mind again, and she winced every time she came to the part where they started yelling... she knew Valiant had left that book there on purpose; she knew he'd be upset. She shouldn't have picked a fight.

By the time they got to Headmaster Emmerson's office, Twila was thoroughly ashamed of herself. What had she been thinking, acting that way?

"I'm sorry—" she started, but Headmaster Emmerson lifted his hand.

"Both of you sit down."

Twila took the nearest chair as Valiant shuffled to the further one. His head was bowed, too, and Twila wondered if he regretted the argument or just regretted being caught.

The two headmasters took their own seats behind the huge oaken desk. Headmaster Olivia folded her hands on the desk, watching the two of them with a grim look in her eye that Twila didn't like. She had interacted little with the headmaster witch since she herself was a dragon. But what she had seen led her to believe Headmaster Olivia was a jovial woman.

"Twila and Valiant," Headmaster Emmerson said, his voice harsher than normal. "Your behavior these last few months has been abhorrent. I am extremely disappointed in both of you."

Twila flinched. There was no point in blaming Valiant for this... she had been instigating just as many arguments as he had.

"Despite your exceptional academic performance, you have proven that you can't work together," Headmaster Olivia continued.

Headmaster Emmerson leaned forward. "Your constant fighting has disrupted the entire school. The second-year students were all in tears before the ceremony, terrified that they'd end up like the two of you."

"We understand this isn't what you wanted," Headmaster Olivia said, her tone softening. "But you have been deliberately antagonizing each other for years now. It's unacceptable. As such, we have decided not to allow your graduation."

Shock rippled through Twila as she stiffened. "Not... but why? We don't have to work together. We can—"

"You are both wonderful students, and your antagonism toward each other is out of character for both of you," Headmaster Olivia interrupted. "We are keeping you over the summer so we can observe you closer. Either you will learn to work together as a team, or at the end of summer, your fated bond will be broken."

Valiant growled. "That's not fair! It's our choice to make."

"And you consider this relationship you have now to be a healthy expression of the bond?" Headmaster Emmerson asked, arching a single eyebrow.

Valiant slumped into his seat. "I have to go home. I'm not staying here; you can't make me."

"We have already contacted your parents. They agree it's best if you stay the summer," Headmaster Olivia concluded.

Twila opened her mouth, but everything about this situation was slowly sinking into her. Their arguments had spilled over; it wasn't just about the two of them anymore. The second-years in tears over having to go through the ceremony? That wasn't right.

"I'm sorry," she mumbled miserably.

"And we hope you can use that sorrow to change your behavior," Headmaster Olivia said.

Headmaster Emmerson got to his feet. "You both may return to your dorm now. However, if we hear that you have been fighting more, we'll have you cleaning out the chicken coop. Understood?"

Twila nodded as she stood. Part of her wanted to turn on Valiant with more blame, but that wouldn't be genuine, and it wouldn't help their situation, either. So, she was silent as she headed out of the office...

Might as well unpack her things again. It was going to be a long summer.

CHAPTER
THREE

"The first week was the hardest. First, all of our classmates graduated, and we were left sitting in the audience." Twila shook her head as she remembered. "I did my best to ignore Valiant. And then the other students left.*

Twila paced from one end of her shared dormitory to the next. Over the past week, all her classmates had packed up their things and moved on with their lives... all the while, she was stuck here, uncertain what she and Valiant were supposed to do over the summer to prove they could get along.

She had made so many plans for the summer! Yes, she knew it was impossible to do everything, but she had fun trying to plan it out.

"All I wanted was one summer with no responsibilities before I figured out where I was going next," she complained aloud to the empty room. Of her two roommates, one had already moved out, and the second was leaving tomorrow.

As her gaze lingered on the enormous trunk at the end of her bed, the weight of the situation settled in. Trapped. That's what she was. She was trapped here because Valiant couldn't be gracious enough to ignore her over the past few months.

Right, because it's all his fault, Twila thought sarcastically, but her self-awareness only made her mood darken further.

The door opened, and she jumped, but it was only Rita, her roommate. Rita's silvery hair was pulled into a bun at the back of her head, and she pushed her glasses up, looking at Twila nervously as though expecting Twila to explode at her.

Twila forced herself to smile in a friendly way, erasing the cloud of doom hanging over her head. "You must be excited about tomorrow."

"Well, I guess," Rita mumbled. "I'm heading off to the Medical Academy. I've got to get started if I'm going to meet the deadline for emissions."

The Medical Academy. "You're going to make a wonderful healer," Twila told her.

"Thanks. And are you going to be all right? I mean, being stuck here all summer?"

Twila wanted to scowl but kept the same bright smile on her face. "Oh, it'll all be fine. One more summer, then I'll be free to go do whatever it is that will bring me joy."

"Are you hoping to break your bond with Valiant?" Rita asked, sitting on the foot of her bed.

Twila didn't answer. Truthfully, that was one thing she had been trying very hard not to think about. Breaking the mating bond wasn't something to be taken lightly... and she didn't want the headmasters to make that choice for her. So what if she and Valiant were always fighting? Why should anyone else get a say in what they did?

"Yeah, I bet you're going to have a great time at the Medical Academy," she said instead, heading for her own bed. "Wow, it's late. I completely lost track of time... goodnight!"

Twila flung herself into her bed and pulled the covers tight around her. The day's events really should have left her exhausted, but her mind kept racing. It wasn't fair. Why did she have to be paired with Valiant all those years ago? What had the stars been thinking?

Howard would have been much better for me, she thought as she rolled to her side.

A pang hit her in the stomach. Three years ago, she had her entire future planned. She and Howard had promised one another that they would have been fated mates. They knew it was the stars that decided these things, but they had been so certain if they proved their devotion to each other strongly enough, the stars would give them what they wanted.

She closed her eyes as she remembered the way Howard used to make her laugh, the way they would cause mischief together, and how utterly betrayed she had felt when she went through the ceremony, only to find herself connected with Valiant.

Howard had ended up with Jessica.

Howard would have been better for me, but Jessica was best for him, Twila continued thinking. Those traitorous tears were pricking her eyes again. There had to be something wrong with her that she couldn't be with the person she wanted.

Instead, she was with Valiant.

And Howard and Jessica were so happy together. They were already planning their wedding, of all things. They were perfect, earning top marks in everything they worked together for.

Twila couldn't find it in herself to be angry at either of them... it wasn't as though they had made the choice, after all. She was jealous, of course. But the fact that they were so perfectly suited for each other made her feel just a little better... at least she was able to be happy for Howard, after all. And Jessica was so sweet, Twila couldn't hate her.

Oh, but if she didn't get her mind on something else, she was going to end up crying. Crying! Over something that happened three years ago, over something that she couldn't change at all.

And if there was one thing Twila knew, it was that this wasn't worth crying over anymore.

"So," she whispered to herself as she sat in the bed, "it's off to the library I go."

She opened the curtain just a touch, making sure it was dark before she slipped out. She pushed her feet into her slippers and pulled on her housecoat before she tiptoed to the door. No sound or movement came from Rita's bed.

The common room was dimly lit, with a light stone lantern on a central table but nothing else. Twila quickly hunted through the books left on the shelves at the side of the room but couldn't find the one she was looking for, so she headed to the library.

The best thing about staying at the Institute over the summer was that the library was never locked up. Reading was highly encouraged, after all.

She was soon in the library, carrying a light stone lantern with her. It swung from her hand as she followed along the familiar shelves until she got to the spot where she knew her favorite book would be located.

She was in luck; it was available. Which, Twila thought, wasn't really that surprising. After all, there weren't many students left at the Institute, and the rooms had been cleaned out already. She picked the book out and headed to a fireplace. This early in summer, the air still had a slight chill to it, but she didn't start a fire.

As she flipped through the pages, a piece of paper dropped into her lap. Twila frowned at it. Had someone left their notes behind?

Setting the book aside, she inspected the paper. It looked ancient; the edges were cracked, and the paper was yellowed. It had that distinctive, slightly musty scent of something that had been hidden away for a long, long time.

"Weird," she murmured as she carefully unfolded the paper. She had read this particular book enough times over the years that it was impossible that she just wouldn't have found it before. Which meant someone had to have recently placed the paper in the book—but why?

As she smoothed out the paper, she found a simple map drawn on it, along with a poem written in a curling script.

A treasure true lies hidden,
Deep within the past unbidden.
Search for me, all who will behold,
An ancient gift of silver and gold.

Twila pursed her lips as she turned it over. A hidden treasure? The map was of the Institute grounds. She'd heard nothing about treasures being kept at the Institute before. So where did this come from, and why was it here now?

"Silver and gold," she muttered, tapping her fingers along the simple map. This here looked like it could be the pond, that would be the training grounds.

She didn't have any need for money. The Crown made sure that all graduates were set up for their future, and Twila was no exception. Although if this treasure was old enough, it would have significant archaeological value. Something that could shed light on their history.

Twila twisted, her book forgotten as she studied the map more deeply. It was something to do, at the very least... A sense of excitement swept through her. *Adventure, here I come!*

CHAPTER
FOUR

aliant laughed fondly. "I also couldn't sleep that night. All my roommates had left already, and since the dorm was all mine now, I had pushed the three beds together, hoping to form one giant bed. I quickly found that no matter how I rearranged the room, my discomfort was too internal to be fixed by changing my surroundings."

The map in Valiant's hand appeared to be changing as he walked. It had taken him some time to figure out it was magical, showing the section of the Institute he was currently in while the little mark that showed where this supposed treasure remained at the corner, as though he hadn't determined the location just yet.

He couldn't sleep, and the dorm was so quiet he thought he might as well try to figure this out. The map came from somewhere, after all. Though he'd found it under the bed where Howard used to sleep, he doubted Howard had left it.

Valian also doubted this treasure even existed. After all, there were dozens of people who lived most of the year here... what were the chances that none of them would have found these clues before now?

On the other hand, the Institute was built on the same grounds as the old palace. If any place had secret passages and hidden treasures, it would be here.

The map led him toward the basement. Normally, these old rooms with their dark stone walls were used only as storage, although it was common for first-years to sneak down here and camp out overnight, telling each other ghost stories.

The mark in the map's corner finally started moving, showing him he was close. As he continued, Valiant suddenly heard muttering ahead of him.

"I'm here; what next?" The voice was distinctly Twila's. As he came to a corner, he dampened the light of his lantern, then peered around the corner. Twila stood at the exact door he wanted to take. "Buried underneath? Is it behind the door? No way has this door never been opened in hundreds of years."

Listening to her growls and mumbles, it soon became painfully clear that Twila was after exactly the same thing as him. How had she found a map? He would have thought she set him up somehow, but he knew that tone too well... she was frustrated, and it wasn't an act.

Valiant hesitated a moment, then shuffled backward. The last thing he needed right now was yet another confrontation with Twila—

His foot kicked something in the dark. A loud hiss and an affronted yowl preceded a sudden clawing sensation across his ankle. Valiant yelled before he could stop himself.

Light blazed around the corner as Twila turned around it. Her eyes widened, then narrowed as she took him in. "You!" she cried accusingly.

Valiant turned on his light again and looked for the cat he had accidentally kicked. It was nowhere in sight. "Me," he grunted.

"You set me up!" Twila crumpled an old-looking piece of paper in her hand. "You... you jerk! It's not bad enough that we're stuck here? You had to leave this phony map for me to find so I'd go on a wild goose chase, didn't you?"

Valiant took a moment to check his ankle. The cat had drawn some blood, but not much. He'd be fine.

Now, about this whole situation. It seemed an unbelievable coincidence that both he and Twila had found a map leading them to the same place at the same time... on the other hand, there were ways of hiding these things with magic. It was possible that an ancient spell was fraying. In which case, Valiant didn't want to share any treasure he found with her.

He shrugged. "All right, you got me. I planted that map. It was easy since you never lock your dorm room."

Twila's silver eyes narrowed further. "Yeah, my dorm. It was clever of you to hide it under my mattress."

Valiant attempted a smirk. "Where else?"

"Liar."

Valiant's head jerked back. "Excuse me?"

"I found it in a book. In the library. And what's that?" Twila lunged, going for the map he held in his own hand. Valiant danced back, holding it behind his back. "You got one, too, didn't you?"

"You're saying you didn't plant it?"

Twila eyed him for a moment. She shoved her map into her dressing gown pocket and shrugged. "Doesn't matter. It's fake, anyway. Why would a treasure be here?"

"Because it used to be a palace," Valiant replied, just to be ornery. Something about contradicting Twila came naturally to him at this point, even though he agreed with her. "I wouldn't be at all surprised if it was real. But go ahead and ignore it... I'll be happy getting all the treasure to myself. Who knows what sort of ancient books could be part of it?"

"Books," Twila repeated, a longing look coming to her face. "That would be magnificent. My riddle talks of silver and gold, though—I thought it was more likely to be ancient artifacts. Maybe death masks."

"That would be amazing, too," Valiant said, getting excited again. "Maybe a relief depicting the first dragon and witch."

"I—" Twila visibly bit down on whatever she was about to say.

Valiant understood—there was no evidence any of this was real. On the other hand, ... He shrugged carelessly as he tucked a strand of his short, silvery hair behind his ear. "If you don't want to look for it, that means the adventure will all be mine."

"You won't find anything. It doesn't exist."

"Maybe not. Maybe it does, though." Valiant grinned at her, a sudden idea popping into his mind as clear as day. "If it does and I find it, then, you will have to do anything I tell you... in front of the entire school."

Twila snorted. "And if you don't find it, you have to do whatever I tell you in front of the entire school... oh, and you have to anyway if I find it first."

"I thought you said it was fake."

"I did, and I'm sure it is. But I can have fun with the treasure hunt all the same, can't I?" Twila gave him a challenging look.

That left him with two possibilities where he was made a fool in front of the school, and only one where Twila was made a fool... and if he was honest, that the treasure wasn't real was most likely... although someone still had to give them both these maps.

He couldn't think of anyone at the Institute who would do this just for laughs. With a grin, he held out his hand. "Deal. Let's shake on it."

Twila took his hand and gave a single, firm pump. Valiant was expecting some sort of macho display from her, squeezing his hand so tight it hurt or some such thing. Instead, he was surprised that she gave him just the right pressure.

"Now. Since we're both here?" Twila gestured toward the door. "Let's see what you come up with."

Valiant strode forward. Whatever his map was leading to was on the other side of the door. "Well, there's no magic on the door at all... so if it's one that wasn't here before, the spell has worn off entirely."

"Do spells do that?"

"Oh, yeah. All the time. Even the most powerful magic can only be traced back to around a thousand years." Valiant glanced over his shoulder. "I'm surprised you don't know that, given how much you love archaeology."

Twila shrugged. "I look more at the cultural details. Not a lot of witches go into archeology, so there isn't a lot of work done on the magical side of things."

"Do dragons...?"

"No," Twila admitted. She leaned against the wall, tossing her long, midnight-black hair over her shoulder. "Guess it's just one of those areas where humans are superiorly suited to. Now the door's locked. Can you unlock it, or should I break it down?"

Valiant touched the lock. His specialty was wordless magic, the sort that could only be felt. The lock was a simple one, easily manipulated. But he hesitated.

"I'm not sure I should. If someone has something private on the other side...."

Twila huffed. "Then I'm going to break it down. Just unlock the door, Valiant."

Valiant hesitated a moment longer before he turned his fingers over the lock, feeling the indescribable feeling of the tumblers against his fingertips. He pushed them in the right order, and the door swung open.

CHAPTER

FIVE

T wila shook her head, a fond smile on her face. "In what shouldn't be a surprise, there was a single box in that room, which contained a single note. A riddle was written on the note, and we quickly figured out that whoever had done this left a series of clues for us to follow. I made a copy of what it said while Valiant kept the original, in case there was magic clinging to it."

A yawn nearly split Twila's jaw as she stumbled into the dining hall. Her eyes were heavy and itchy with tiredness. But she was never one to sleep in late, even when she had stayed up far into the night poring over the latest riddle she'd discovered from the treasure hunt.

The stupid thing would not be solved. She had read it forward, backward, upside down, in a mirror, and many things, but she still hadn't been able to figure it out. Something about the note had to be solvable, but she was stumped.

Most of the tables had been removed from the dining hall since there weren't many students or teachers who stayed at the Institute over the summer. Twila was thankful that the cooking service was still offered, though it had changed to buffet-style rather than individual plates being brought out.

One table remained empty. But as Twila piled food onto her plate, her gaze traveled to where Valiant sat. He was writing something, his own plate of food ignored as he hunched over the paper.

Maybe he had figured something out.

Twila swung her braid over her shoulder and sauntered over to him, sitting close enough to see but far enough for comfort. "You figure something out?"

Valiant jumped as he looked up. His black eyes were ringed with a puffy redness and dark circles and smudges under them. Twila was shocked at how awful he looked.

"Are you okay?" she blurted without thinking.

Valiant's cheeks darkened. "I'm fine," he snapped back.

His notebook sat nearby. He snapped it shut with an extra-loud bang before he bent over his writing again, sliding one of his arms around to block Twila from seeing whatever he had written.

"Um," Twila said, uncertain. Her heart tugged to see the normally unflappable Valiant showing such emotion—okay, maybe he wasn't unflappable, but she still hadn't seen him so clearly upset about anything before. "Oh, you're out of water. You want me to refill your glass? Juice, maybe?"

Valiant gave her a puzzled look and shrugged.

Twila grabbed his glass and hurried over to the buffet table, hating how unnerved she was right now. A strange sort of prickling rose on the back of her neck, no matter how much she fought it. It was the same sort of feeling she used to get in the forest when a predator was nearby.

But there was no danger here at the Institute... it had to be something else.

She returned with the juice and slid back into her chair, studying Valiant's profile. "Are you sure you're okay?"

"It doesn't have anything to do with this treasure hunt, so you don't have to worry about it," Valiant snapped at her.

Twila leaned back in her chair, scowling. She could see that! All she had to do was take one look at him, and she knew it was far more important than this silly bet between them. Did he really think so little of her that everything she said or did was something to get a one-up on him?

A sinking, guilty feeling flooded through her... of course he did. Hadn't that been the basis of their relationship for the last three years? Each of them punishing the other for something that was completely out of their control.

Twila's shoulders slumped forward as her lingering irritation vanished.

"I don't care about the treasure hunt right now," she said, trying to keep her tone fairly neutral. "You don't look so great, and I... I wouldn't say I'm worried, exactly, but it's not like you to be like this... I mean, you obviously had a rough night....."

She trailed off, uncertain how to continue. Shaking her head, she looked away. Talking about emotions and checking up on other people's feelings weren't exactly her strong suit. Give her something to build or fight, sure. Twila could do that easily. Solving problems was easy so long as she could use her hands to fix something.

"Sorry," she mumbled. "I don't know if I'm making it worse or not. I have a hard time with... *people*."

"Never would have guessed that," Valiant replied with a mutter.

Twila poked at her breakfast. "It's why I wanted to be matched with Howard. I could at least understand when he said he was fine, he was fine, and it wasn't just an 'I'm not fine, but I don't want to talk about it' answer."

Valiant laid his pen aside and turned over his paper, so she couldn't read it. "I'm sorry. You're right; I'm not fine. It's just that... it's not something that I want to talk about with you."

He watched her face as though expecting some sort of comeback. Twila only nodded, though; she expected that would be the case, after all.

"Do we need to put a hold on the treasure hunt, then?" she asked, her expression smooth. "Wouldn't want an unfair advantage."

"No. It'll be good to have the distraction." Valiant leaned against the table, staring at his still-untouched food. "I just learned that my grandmother is sick. She's had frail health for a few years now, and they're not sure what this illness is just yet."

Twila's stomach clenched. A sick grandmother? She chewed her lip, struggling to know how to reply to that. What could she say? Nothing fixed that sort of worry. "I'm sorry," she offered quietly. "I hope she gets better quickly."

Valiant picked up his fork but still didn't eat. "I just hate being stuck here."

"Have you talked to the headmasters? Maybe they can make an exception for the circumstances?" Twila leaned forward slightly, intent on Valiant's face.

To her surprise, he answered her concern with a black glare. "Do you think I'm stupid? Of course I've thought about it. You don't have to act as though you're the only person who has the answers, Twila. I know what is going on, and I know what I need to do."

"I'm only trying to help," Twila protested. Where had this hostility come from? She wasn't saying that she'd come up with this brilliant plan he was too dumb to think of. She was asking if he had talked to them yet.

Why would he take her words and immediately assume the worst of her?

"You're impossible," she snapped, grabbing her food. "You don't want to talk? Fine. We won't talk. And at the end of the summer, our fated bond will be broken, and you don't have to worry about me being in your life ever again."

"I never said—"

But Twila wasn't interested in listening any more. She stormed to another table and threw her plate down, then sat and started shoveling the food into her mouth. So what if he didn't want to talk to her? It was his loss. He was the one being an idiot.

Is he, though? The annoying jab of conscience asked. *Or is he just overwhelmed and afraid and lashing out at the easiest target?*

But why should I have to be the one to guide him through his emotions?

He never asked you to... but you could show some compassion.

Twila hid her face in her hands as she tried to silence the conversation in her head. It wasn't her job to show him compassion. It wasn't her job to fix his problems... he wasn't even asking her for help! But maybe, just maybe, he didn't need help. Maybe he just needed someone to talk to.

Someone who understood what it felt like to lose a grandparent.

Her stupid conscience felt like it was feeding the guilt in her chest until she looked up again. No, this wasn't something she could fix, but she had to be logical here. Valiant wasn't asking her for anything. What she could offer was the distraction he needed... somehow.

She took a deep breath and left her plate as she headed back to him. But what could she possibly say?

CHAPTER
SIX

"The truth of the matter was I wanted to talk. I just didn't know how. I'd never dealt with death before in my life, and I had been terrified of losing my grandmother for years already. I just didn't know how to deal with my own emotions. Twila was an easy scapegoat; I'm ashamed to admit. I knew I was wrong to treat her the way I was treating her... it was just easier to feel that anger than admit how deep my fear went."

"I'm sorry."

Valiant looked up. Twila was back, standing just far enough away to make talking awkward. He stared at her blankly, uncertain how to respond to her words. Well, he could tell her to go away again. It was what he wanted to say.

On the other hand, the way she was looking at him, with a wariness to her expression, made his shoulders slump. She expected him to be angry. It irritated him, but also just made him so exhausted...

If he wasn't too tired to fight, he might have snapped at her.

"I really don't want to talk," Valiant grumbled, unable to keep the emotion from his voice.

"I know. I just wanted to say sorry... I lost my grandmother a few years back. So, I know it hurts. Um... yeah. I guess, uh, I'll just... let you gather your stuff up and then steal your notebook? So, then you can chase me and not have to... think?"

Valiant stared at her. What was she going on about?

Twila rubbed her forehead. "Yeah. I'm just making this worse. I'll just go away."

She turned on her heel, but Valiant wasn't ready for her to leave—no, he didn't want to talk, at least not about his family situation, but he also didn't understand what was going on in her head... and he didn't like it.

"Come back," he said, standing. "Why are you stealing my notebook?"

Twila turned back to him, blushing. Somehow, the pink flush to her cheeks made her look younger. He'd never thought she looked old, but it never occurred to him that Twila really was the same age as he was. She'd always seemed to possess a self-assurance that made her seem more mature or something.

"The thought was, I grab it and make you chase me all over the Institute," Twila said, twitching. "When I lost my grandma, doing physical activity always helped. Gave me something to occupy my hands, and when it was hard enough, it would occupy my mind, too."

Valiant felt a lump rise in his throat. "So, what you're saying is you want to get me running all over the place, so I don't have to think?"

"Uh... yeah. But it's stupid; you're not me. I'm sure you have other plans."

"I have my chores," Valiant said. He tried to pull in some anger toward Twila, tried to convince himself that she was interfering in a way to win the bet... but she looked so uncharacteristically nervous he couldn't bring himself to think it was anything but genuine. "And I probably ought to get some studying done."

"Right. So, I'll just leave you."

"Uh—" Valiant blurted, unable to stop himself. His cheeks flamed as Twila stopped once more. Why was this so difficult? "Actually, part of it was that I wanted to work on the obstacle course."

Twila's eyebrows pinched together. "But you're a witch. You don't need to do that."

"I plan on joining the Quake Watch. I need to have physical abilities, so I can deal with any situations that come up." Valiant stared at his hands.

"Oh. Oh, well... I can help with that. I'll set up the nets while you do your chores and talk with the headmasters."

Valiant frowned at her.

Twila lifted her hands. "I'm not trying to tell you what to do or suggest that I'm smarter than you. What I mean is, after thinking about it, I can understand you haven't had the chance to talk to them yet. And they'll for sure say you can go home. If we end up having to spend the autumn semester here...."

Valiant opened his mouth, irritation spiking through him, but he shut it quickly. As much as he would like to fight right now, just to stop himself from having to think and feel about everything that seemed to be going wrong, Twila was just trying to help. In her clumsy way, yeah, but he could appreciate the effort she was putting into this.

"I'll be at the course at noon," he said instead.

"Right. All right, I'll have everything ready."

Twila scurried away quickly, and Valiant watched her go, uncertain what this weighty feeling in his chest was. He should feel grateful to her, shouldn't he? But something just... everything seemed to be wrong, and he didn't know how to deal with it.

So, he turned back to his letter, signed his name, and began folding it.

He would not deal with it, not yet. Talk to the headmasters. Do his chores. Then meet Twila at the obstacle course and burn off this energy.

And this whole treasure hunt thing... well, if Twila was using his distraction to get a leg up on him, he didn't care. It only proved what a petty person she actually was if that was what she was doing. If she wasn't being genuine.

If she was genuine in trying to help him out... that brought up whole additional issues. Like, issues that stated he wasn't as impartial as he thought he was and that these past three years of constant squabbles were all his fault.

It was several hours later that Valiant finally came to the obstacle course. Talking to the headmasters had taken out a lot more from him than he expected, but he would head home for a week soon. Chores completed, he only came to the course because Twila was waiting for him.

And right now, the last thing he wanted was more fighting.

Which was odd since so often he sought Twila out specifically to pick a fight.

"Hey," Valiant greeted Twila as he came to the advanced courses. She had set up the nets and pulled out the mats. Valiant's heart sank as he looked over it. "I, uh... I've changed my mind. I'm too tired to run the course."

Twila scooted over on the low wooden platform she sat on. "Pop a squat and let's look at the last riddle, then. I can't figure it out."

"Pop a squat?" Variant repeated incredulously.

"Yeah. Sit down."

"Doesn't that mean emptying the bowels in the forest?"

Twila laughed. "No! It means sitting down. Now come on. Sit down and help me figure this out. I've tried everything to read this stupid riddle, and I can't get it."

She waved a paper toward him. Valiant considered pointing out that they were supposed to be competing with this, but she could have gotten angry with him for making her set all this up when he had changed his mind...

So, he 'popped a squat' and sat next to her on the platform. As Valiant read her riddle, his brow furrowed. The paper looked as old as everything that they had found so far. It was clearly torn on the right side, missing important information.

"Where did you find this?"

"Under the floorboards in the second-floor toilets."

"Huh." Valiant pulled a paper from his pocket and showed it to her. It was torn down the left side. "I found this under the floorboards in the first-floor toilets. And look, they fit perfectly together."

He placed the two pieces together. As he did so, the words on both sides rearranged themselves, becoming clear.

"Oh," Twila breathed as she leaned in. "So we needed both sides to read it... what a coincidence," she added dryly. When Valiant looked up at her, she gave him a knowing look.

"I didn't set this up," he protested.

"Never said you did."

Valiant huffed and rolled his eyes. He wasn't interested in figuring out what she was thinking. "Hold on and let me write this down."

He scribbled down his notes as Twila did the same. They each silently studied the new clue for a while before Valiant carefully took his side back. The words became a jumbled mess once more as he tucked it into his notebook.

"Guess you're going to have a head start on this one... I'm heading back home tomorrow," Valiant said, turning his face to the warm summer sun.

It felt good, that warmth on his skin. He loved everything about summer. But this year at the Institute, it all felt painfully slow. Hope-fully, some good, hard labor back home would help him get out of this strange mood he found himself in.

Labor and seeing for myself how bad Grandma is. The not knowing was the worst part. If she was terribly sick, wouldn't his parents have asked him to come home? But if she wasn't terribly sick, why did they say she was 'very' ill?

"You're going home?" Twila asked.

"I talked with the headmasters, and they said it was all right."

"Oh." Twila kicked her feet off the platform. "Good. I hope you have a pleasant visit. I'm going to put away this stuff now."

She hopped off the platform, leaving Valiant confused as she stared after her. Why the sudden change in mood? He sighed as he shook his head... just one more reason they weren't suited for each other. He never knew what Twila was thinking.

A pang hit his stomach, and he didn't know what it meant... so he ignored the feeling and helped put away the supplies.

CHAPTER
SEVEN

Twila rocked her feet on the ground, making the bench swing lightly back and forth. "I don't remember what I was thinking. I knew it was best for you to go home. I don't think I wanted an invitation, not at that time. Anyway, the next few weeks were boring. The only other students were much younger than me, and of course, the headmasters were so much older. I missed Valiant. More than I could have admitted to anyone, especially myself."

Twila jerked awake at the sound of a door closing. She quickly sat up from where she was sprawled out on a sitting couch, wiping the corner of her mouth that accumulated spittle. A yawn stretched across her jaw as she stretched her back.

"Sorry, I didn't mean to wake you," Valiant said as he pulled his heavy trunk toward his room.

Twila jumped to her feet. "You're back!"

"I'm back. You knew I was only going to be gone for three weeks."

Twila glanced around the common room and blushed. She had certainly allowed herself to take over... her mess was everywhere. Quickly, she gathered things up. "Don't look; I meant to clean this up before you got back. I thought I had tonight and tomorrow left."

Valiant paused in his doorway and gave a small chuckle. "I'll give you a few minutes, I suppose, while I put my things away."

Good. That gave her time enough to put the room back into some semblance of order. Twila dashed about the common room, grabbing her piles of mess to chuck into her dorm instead. She'd take care of everything tomorrow.

By the time Valiant returned to the common room, she'd tidied everything up and was dusting down the mantle. Valiant seemed surprised at how much she had accomplished as he went over to a table.

A frown crossed over his face. "Are these your notes on the treasure hunt?"

Twila glanced over her shoulder. "Uh, yeah."

"You haven't gotten very far."

Twila came over to straighten up the papers. "It didn't seem fair since you were going to be so busy with your family."

She waited, uncertain if she should ask about his grandmother or wait for him to speak. Valiant seemed to be calmer, more rested than he had been when he left. Valiant stretched out his back and gestured toward the door.

"Want to go for a walk? I'm all stiff from riding in the carriage."

Twila was pleasantly surprised by the suggestion. "Sure. You want any snacks before we head out?"

Valiant shook his head.

They headed outside and started toward the pond. It was well past dark, but the light stones on the path made it easy to cross. The air was still and cool, a relief after the hot day. Twila inhaled deeply, reminding herself to open the windows when they returned to the dorms.

"How is your grandmother doing?" she finally asked.

"Better. Not as good as I'd like, but as good as can be expected," Valiant replied. "She's a stubborn old lady, but she is getting older every year. I know it's inevitable... I just don't want it to happen."

Twila slid her hand into his, squeezing lightly. The warmth of his hand around hers was pleasant. Even after he squeezed back, she didn't let him go. They sauntered around the pond; Twila would have liked to go faster but made herself allow Valiant to set the pace.

"So. How have you been?" Valiant asked. "Were you able to get any of your summer plans completed?"

"Nah. Three weeks isn't even long enough for me to fly everywhere I want to visit. I suppose I could have gone to the Golden Forest, but it almost seemed like a waste of time," Twila shrugged.

She had considered asking the headmasters for a break herself, but without Valiant around, there was extra work to be done. She had done her best to help and take on his chores alone with her own. Boring, yes, but life wasn't all about having fun.

"The Golden Forest, huh?" Valiant asked.

Twila smiled. "Remember our second year? The Chameleon Sprites were so much fun to spend time with. I've been wanting to go back and hang out for some time. But I had a lot of other places I wanted to go, too. I guess I'll just have to plan to do it next year."

She kicked a small rock toward Valiant's feet. He kicked it back, and she caught it with the side of her foot and dribbled it between her feet sometime before passing it back to him.

"I'd love to travel like that," Valiant said as he moved the rock around with his feet. "Maybe someday. I have too many responsibilities at home, though. And with my grandma in her state, I don't want to be off gallivanting if...."

Twila squeezed his hand again.

Valiant cleared his throat. "Anyway. Grandma is doing better, and that's what I need to focus on. I figured out the next step of the puzzle. I thought you'd be working on it, so I kept at it. But since you weren't working on it, I might as well share... it's only fair."

It took Twila a moment to catch up with his sudden change in conversation. She wanted to say something, offer some words of comfort considering his grandmother's health, but even she could tell when someone didn't want to talk about something so obvious.

There was only so much that words could do, anyway, especially since Valiant had lost no one before. One of her first memories was the confusion and sadness that was grief... she couldn't imagine having to fear it so terribly, not knowing its sting.

"Right. So, uh, you figured out the clue?" she asked, attempting a bright tone.

"It's why I suggested we take this walk. Come on." He tugged her hand as he broke into a trot, pulling her along.

They went to the old stables, which were currently undergoing some cosmetic renovations. The original walls were exposed, and Valiant led her to the far wall.

"The riddle said something about golden horses," he said. "We need to look for a brick that looks blond or has a horse sketched onto it—"

"Like this one?" Twila asked, pointing. Right at the top of the wall was a stone carved into the shape of a horse's head. She lifted it and weighed it in her hands. "It's far too light to be full stone. Oh!" Her eyes lit up as she hurried closer to one of the hanging light stones. "It's a puzzle box!"

Valiant groaned. "I hate puzzle boxes."

"I love them," Twila said, engrossed.

She felt along the edges and tested pulling or pushing various parts of the carved statue. After a few minutes, she figured out she needed to press both eyes and pull on the left ear at the same time.

The horse's mouth opened, and a curled piece of paper fell out. With a cry of triumph, she snatched up the paper and smoothed it out... only to find that it was utterly blank.

"What is this?" she demanded, affronted. Did they really spend all this time on a treasure hunt just to find that whoever put it together had quit in the laziest of fashions? "Look at this!"

Valiant laughed, and for a second, Twila was certain he was pulling a prank on her. Luckily, he spoke before she could start spitting accusations. "It's got a spell on it. Look, you can see the sheen when you tilt it."

He demonstrated, and Twila did, in fact, see a slight unnatural glow emanating off it. "Can you take the spell off?"

"Oh, yeah. This is a simple process... It'll take a couple of days to get the potion brewed, though. I have to be careful if I don't want to destroy what's under the spell."

A couple of days. Twila grinned. Yeah, she could wait. The fun was just getting started again.

EIGHT

"*I*t was too late to start the potion right away, and besides that, I really was exhausted. We agreed that we'd get up early the next morning to start the potion. I ended up sleeping in," Valiant chuckled. "That's the one thing we still argue about, isn't it?"

Valiant glanced up from where he was sweeping to check on Twila. She was scrubbing down the dining hall tables. It was their job this week to make sure the dining hall remained clean. And since he had ended up in bed until almost noon, they'd had to start their chores instead of working on the potion like Twila wanted.

To his surprise, though, she was crooning to herself as she moved from table to table.

"You're not still mad at me, are you?" he asked finally.

Twila shrugged. "You've had a long journey. It makes sense that you needed extra rest."

Her tone said that she was making a deliberate effort not to pick a fight, though, and Valiant found himself smiling at that. "After we're done here, I can start gathering up what I'll need. I think I'm on cleaning the chicken coop this week, but—"

"Oh, I already did that," Twila interrupted.

Valiant looked up in surprise, leaning on his broom. "What?"

"I looked at your chores and did all the ones you need to do today while you were sleeping. Better to get it done, and then you could start on the potion rather than waiting and waiting, right?" Twila asked brightly.

"But that's a lot," Valiant protested. "I could have started the potion first."

Twila shrugged as she lifted the chairs onto the table so he could sweep around it. "As I said, it was better than just waiting. Besides, I don't mind it so much. I've got this story I tell myself when I'm doing unpleasant tasks. Makes it nicer."

Valiant watched her for a moment, impressed by how quickly she moved. A stab of guilt shot through him as he remembered how dismissive he had been of her over the past three years. Whenever they had ended up with their tasks together, he'd taken any of her attempts to sing, chat, or play while working as a waste of time.

He'd been so focused on his own disappointment he hadn't really stopped to consider how all of this affected her.

He resumed sweeping. "Twila?"

"Yeah?"

"This might be the wrong time, but I just wanted to let you know... I'm sorry that you didn't get Howard for your mate. And I'm sorry that I haven't been the best partner." Valiant kept his eyes down.

Part of him still didn't believe that he should apologize. After all, it wasn't his fault that they'd been paired... but he couldn't look at it that way any longer. He should have shown her long before now that he was sympathetic to her not getting the mate she wanted. Should have behaved much differently... In fact, that was one thing he knew he did need to apologize for.

"My behavior over these last three years has been awful," he continued. "I blamed you for everything even when I knew it was not your doing any more than you losing the relationship you had with Howard was my fault. I've been deliberately picking fights with you so that I wouldn't have to deal with... anything, really."

Silence answered him. Valiant kept working, a new sort of tension in the air. He was used to angry tension, but this was... something else entirely. He wasn't sure what it was. Anxiety? Vulnerability? Something else?

"Thank you," Twila said eventually. "And I'm sorry for how I acted, too. I saw how disappointed you were when we were paired, and I took it personally."

"It was personal, even though it wasn't your fault," Valiant admitted. "I think part of it was because I was convinced you didn't like me... or maybe I was afraid you wouldn't like me. I don't know... maybe I'm just making excuses now."

It felt strange to be so open and honest about his feelings those many years ago. And, if he was honest, Valiant wasn't sure he entirely remembered everything he'd felt. Surely, there was plenty that he'd convinced himself he felt afterward, the way kids do.

"I did like you. Actually, if I hadn't thought I was in love with Howard at the time, I probably would have been happy to have you as my match," Twila said. She had moved to the next table, scrubbing it thoroughly with her head bent, but Valiant still saw her ears turning pink.

She had liked him?

"You thought you loved him?" Valiant probed cautiously.

Twila shrugged, turning her body, so her back was to him. "Yeah, well. I was fifteen. That's too young to actually be in love; you have no idea what it really is."

"I was in love."

Twila peeked over her shoulder. "I don't—" She rubbed her temples with her fingertips. "From my perspective... you were in love as much as fifteen-year-olds can be in love. It could have turned into true love eventually, but I just don't think that children are capable of loving in the same way adults do."

"That doesn't mean that love isn't real."

Twila shrugged her shoulders. "Guess I'm just talking about me, then. I wasn't in love with Howard because I did not know what love actually was."

Valiant considered her words as he swept the pile of crumbs and dirt into a dustpan. While he did want to argue further about this, did it really matter? Clearly, they were coming at the issue from two different points of view... did he really want to ruin their budding relationship to prove he was 'right' over something like this?

"Does that mean you think fifteen is too young for the matching ceremony?" he asked, just because he was curious. There was no other reason.

"I think... we put too much emphasis on the romantic potential of fated mates," Twila replied, sounding cautious. "As though fated mates who aren't romantically in love have something missing."

Valiant found himself with nothing left to sweep, so he retrieved the mop and started at the furthest corner. "I guess I understand where you're coming from. I've never thought of it that way."

"It doesn't have to be romantic, and romance isn't the most important part of being fated mates, either," Twila continued. She tossed her rag into the soapy bucket and turned to him, her shoulders tense, her silvery eyes sharp. "Do you want romance? We might still break our bond, but if we don't... do you want romance with... your fated mate?

Valiant's face heated as his throat went dry. Twila's direct honesty was something he both admired and dreaded. He should have known this was coming, and yet it hadn't ever occurred to him that she might have different ideas of what she wanted from this...

Whatever sort of relationship they had.

"I always assumed I would have a romantic relationship with my fated mate," Valiant said slowly, not daring to look at Twila as he spoke.

He started trying to imagine what romance with Twila would look like and quickly stomped it out—they weren't even friends, and he couldn't think of things like kissing, marriage, children... Not with her, at least. Valiant had always been solid in the knowledge he needed to like someone before he was attracted to them.

He hadn't allowed himself to like Twila in a long time.

"I'm not sure a romantic relationship would be possible between you and me," he continued, knowing that he needed to be totally honest with her. "But at the same time, the idea that the headmasters could just make us break our bond... I don't like it."

"I know what you mean," Twila murmured.

Valiant rolled his shoulders, trying to loosen his tight muscles. "If they asked, it would be one thing."

"I don't like being told what to do," Twila said. "I don't like that choice being made for me."

"Yeah. Exactly."

Valiant finally looked up and met Twila's gaze. There was deep emotion in her eyes, an emotion he couldn't read. It was something that drew him in, though. He wanted to reassure her, but reassure her of what?

They silently returned to work. Valiant's thoughts raced, but he didn't know what to say, so he remained silent.

CHAPTER
NINE

"The truth of the matter, of course," Twila drawled, "was that I very much wanted my fated mate. I wanted a romantic relationship with my fated mate. I had mistakenly assumed that once I had my mate, everything would be perfect, and we'd just instantly love each other. My rejection of Valiant was entirely connected to that. I felt like something of a failure because he didn't love me instantly... and I felt broken because I didn't love him instantly. I wish I had known then what I know now. Love isn't something you just get. Love is something that you nurture."

Twila carefully erased a single spot on her charcoal drawing, intently adding the slightest bit of shine to the shadow.

Valiant entered the room, and Twila had the instant urge to hide her art but forced herself not to. It wasn't as though he cared about what she did as a hobby.

"The potion's ready. I—oh, wow," he said, coming to stand behind her. Valiant peered at her picture so intently that Twila blushed. A smile spread over his face. "You have a real good eye for composition."

Twila closed her sketchbook. Somehow the compliment was even more embarrassing than if he'd insulted her. "It's just an apple."

"Yeah, but you got the shading and shape and all that really well."

Twila cleared her throat, blushing. "You said the potion was ready? Let's get that map, then."

"We don't know if it's actually a map," Valiant mentioned, but he laid the paper on the table and smoothed it out. Then, he produced a small vial from his pocket and dripped a single drop on the paper.

Twila leaned in close, watching as the page shimmered, then lines appeared. It spread out from the center, like a drop of water spreading through tissue paper. She was right; it was a map. The lines were simple and rough, just like the original map she had discovered.

Unlike that one, however, even after the whole thing was revealed, she had no idea what anything on it was.

"Could this be the pond?" she asked, poking a circular shape with her forefinger.

"Uuuh... I don't think so. If it was, then the Institute would have to be around here, and the messenger hawks would be over here," Valiant replied, pointing.

"Maybe it's not to scale?"

Valiant shook his head. "No, whoever put this together has been too careful about that. I just... oh!" he straightened and grabbed a pencil. "Can I see a blank page in your book?"

Twila stiffened but cautiously flipped to the back of her sketchbook and passed it over. Valiant made a few rough lines on the page, mimicking the basics of the map. Then, he added in a few more lines, and slowly Twila could start to see it come into place.

"It's a map of the third floor!" she exclaimed. She peered closer as the circles and strange wiggles became clearer. "There are the stairs, that's the atrium, and that right there... what is that?"

"That," Valiant said, tapping the page where she was pointing, "is the fountain in the atrium. I bet that's where we have to go next. Let's go!"

He jumped to his feet with the map clutched tightly in one hand. Twila grabbed her notebook and pencil, leaving the sketchbook behind as they raced to the third floor.

The atrium was a beautiful, open space. Raised garden beds scattered across the floor, lined by paths paved in stone to mimic the appearance of an outdoor walk. Plants from all over the world were grown here, and the different areas were separated magically to mimic the biomes the plants were from. Twila had often retreated here and hidden among the foliage to read on rainy days."

The fountain was in the atrium's part that reflected the flora from Odentia, a neighboring kingdom. It sat in the middle of a large indoor pond with lily pads and duckweed blossoming in it. Low juniper bushes and towering redwood cedars surrounded them.

Valiant circled the pond. "I guess we'll have to wade into the fountain."

"I'm just glad there are no fish in there," Twila said as she stripped off her shoes and socks.

She rolled up her pant legs and carefully slipped her feet into the fountain. The atrium being temperature controlled meant it was pleasant to be in, and the cool water sent a pleasant shiver running up her spine.

Valiant waded in from the other side, and they met at the fountain. It was simply made, three bowls getting progressively bigger until the biggest overflowed into the pond.

As Twila peered into the top of the fountain, she found... nothing. Her heart froze, then dropped. She searched the sides of the fountain, then up and down in the pond, but there was nothing. No inscriptions, no papers, no hidden compartments. Valiant searched with her, neither of them speaking.

It couldn't end like this. It just couldn't. It wasn't fair! After all the effort they had put into this treasure hunt, they couldn't just end up without further answers.

And, if she were honest with herself, Twila didn't want the treasure hunt to end. She sat on the edge of the pond, hiding her face in her hands. It had given her and Valiant something to work together on. Over these last few weeks, they had gotten along. They might even have been moving toward friendship!

Twila liked the way they worked together on this. She liked the possibility of finding common ground...

She liked the idea that maybe breaking their bond wasn't their only option. Maybe if they just allowed themselves to set aside their preju-dices and hurt feelings, they might figure out a way to make this work. Maybe they weren't destined for romance, but maybe there really was a reason the stars put them together.

"I don't get it," Valiant said as he gave up and sat next to her. "It should be here."

It should be, but it wasn't. Twila fought the lump rising in her throat. Instead, she straightened herself. "Let me see the map again. Maybe we misread it."

"Maybe," Valiant said, but the doubt was clear in his voice.

He handed the map over to Twila, and she studied it. The small circles were classrooms, the squiggles were stairs, and this oval shape with waves in it was clearly water. The fountain. Were there any other places here on the third floor that had water?

"Water," she whispered. Excitement coursed through her as she plunged her hand and the map beneath the surface of the fountain.

"Hey!" Valiant shouted. He grabbed at the map, and Twila released it at once to avoid tearing it. "What are you—"

Valiant cut out as he lifted the paper from the fountain water. His eyes widened. Twila leaned in to find color had blossomed over the page, presenting an entirely new image. She laughed and jumped to her feet, punching the air.

"I knew it! The fountain was drawn far bigger than it should be. The rest of it is roughly to scale but not the fountain. So, I figured it out; we needed water from the fountain to reveal the next clue!" She struck a pose, one hand on her hip, as she jutted it out and fluffed her midnight hair with her other hand. "You may praise my intelligence if you wish."

"You could have told me what you were doing first," Valiant grum-bled. He stepped from the fountain's pond. "What if you had been wrong? You could have ruined our map!"

"But I wasn't wrong."

"But you could have been."

Twila frowned as she stepped from the fountain and kicked her feet to dry them faster. "I wasn't."

Valiant laid the wet paper on the side of the fountain and glared at her. "That's not the point. The point is that you decided to take action without even talking about it with me. It was a decision we should have made *together*."

"I... didn't think of it that way. I'm sorry."

Valiant sighed. "You were right, though. So, I guess I'm sorry for getting so angry. Anyway. This new map... that's the pond, isn't it?"

Twila bent to study the new, colorful rendition of the map. "Yes, it is. Guess we're going swimming, huh?"

CHAPTER

TEN

Valiant wrinkled his nose as he remembered how long it had taken them to search the pond. They'd spent days diving into it and figuring out different ways to crawl along the bottom. Of course, they were eventually successful.

"As soon as we went diving into the pond and found the strongbox that was shown on our new box, I knew that this was no ancient treasure hunt. I'd always suspected, but this was proof. The pond had only been put in thirty years previously. There was no way an ancient treasure could have been buried there. But I was having too much fun to start letting logic get the better of me now."

The contents of the strongbox were spread over the table in the common room. A few coins, some papers, a magically protected book he couldn't open. He knew it all had to mean something, but he had no clue just yet.

Twila came into the common room from her dorm, toweling off her long, dark hair. Valiant's own silver hair was slicked back. He hadn't bothered doing anything with it besides brushing it.

"Trying to get a head start on the next leg of the journey so you can beat me?" she teased.

"Beat... oh." Valian laughed. He had forgotten all about their bet.

Twila twisted her damp hair into a bun at the back of her head, revealing her long neck. Valiant watched as a single drop of water ran down it before he realized what he was doing and quickly tore his eyes away.

"So, have you found anything?" Twila asked as she joined him.

"I haven't put it together yet, no," he said. "There might be another puzzle in the strongbox, but I couldn't sense any magic on it. I thought maybe we should head down and get some food before we try to figure it out."

Twila picked up one coin and turned it over in her fingers. "Probably a good idea. You missed breakfast."

Valiant's eyebrows shot straight up, disappearing into his silvery hair. "What?"

"You missed breakfast," Twila repeated.

"How do you know that?"

Twila gave him a withering glance. "Maybe because you weren't there, the cooks cleaned up, and then I found you cleaning out the stables. So, unless you went to the kitchen directly...."

Valiant scowled, more because he didn't like being called out for missing a meal than anything else. The fact that Twila noticed gave him a certain fuzzy, warm feeling in his chest. "Well, you snuck dessert into your room last night at midnight."

"Hey!" Twila swatted his arm playfully. "You were sleeping!"

"I was sitting beside the fire, reading. You just didn't notice me."

Twila covered her mouth with her hand, stifling a laugh.

Valiant grinned back and stood, offering his arm. Twila took it, and they headed down to the dining hall.

"It was chocolate cake," Twila whispered to him after they left the dorms. "Next time, I'll bring you some, too."

"I'll ask the cooks to make coconut cookies," Valiant whispered back. "They're your favorite, right?"

Twila smacked her lips together. "For sure!"

They collected their plates of food and, since it was such a lovely day out, took their meals to eat on the grass. They talked about desserts first, a little about the treasure, but mostly about the book that Twila convinced Valiant to read; he was pleased to say it was his new obsession.

Once they were finished eating, Valiant stretched out of the grass and pillowed his head on his hands. "I'm glad the headmasters stopped us from graduating. This summer has been... a lot. But it's been good."

Twila lay down next to him, her eyes shut. "Yeah. It really has been. And I'm glad we're not fighting anymore. Or at least, when we do fight, we talk about it."

"Yeah."

Valiant licked his lips, feeling nervous suddenly. "Um... Twila?"

"Mmm?"

"Can we talk about fated mates? And what we are going to do?"

Twila opened her eyes again. "I don't know if I can talk about that without starting a fight."

"Mostly, I want to say some things... if it's okay."

"I don't know if it's okay until you say it. So I guess go ahead." She closed her eyes again, but this time Valiant could see the creases at the corners of her eyes, telling him she was pinching her lids shut a little too tightly.

Valiant collected his thoughts and set them in order before he spoke. "I don't want to break our bond. Not now that we have got along. We talked before about the assumption of romance in fated mates, and I don't want that assumption to ruin the friendship we could have."

Twila nodded slightly, showing she was still listening.

"My uncle is a dragon, and he and his fated mate don't have a romantic relationship. I've been writing to him, and I think maybe that's where it went wrong, at least on my part. I was forcing the idea of a romantic relationship on you when neither of us was ready for one. When I should have been thinking of you as my best friend rather than the ideal woman."

Twila was silent. What was she thinking? Did she find anything in his monologue that she agreed with? Was she waiting for him to say more... did she need the silence to formulate her own thoughts?

"The point of being fated mates is that we're supposed to complement each other, to form a perfect working pair for the betterment of the Kingdom," Valiant continued. "And I—"

"Valiant?"

"Yes?"

Twila pushed herself into a sitting position, clasping her hands over her knees. "You're not the only one. To push that assumption onto our relationship. I thought that my fated mate would just love me automatically, and somehow because he loved me, I would overcome all my flaws."

Valiant opened his mouth and closed it again. That wasn't how it worked! But Twila had to know that wasn't how it worked. So he had to say something to comfort her... or did he need to acknowledge her feelings?

"I... don't think our flaws are there to be fixed," he finally said, wincing as he did so.

"No? You don't think we should try to fix them?"

"Strengthen them, sure. But fix makes it sound like you're inherently broken because you're flawed... I don't think that's right." He shuffled their dirty dishes into a pile. "Besides, what you see as a flaw might be something someone else sees as a strength."

Twila snorted. "Oh, you mean like my immaturity?"

"Actually... yeah."

"You're joking."

Valiant shook his head. He had thought that Twila understood exactly what she was doing with all of her playful acting. "I'm serious. You call it being immature, and yeah, sometimes I agree with you, but you also turn things into games. Remember when we were going to the Silver Springs?"

Twila gave him a searching look. "Yeah, of course I do."

"You had us all singing as we trekked up that mountain," Valiant said, laughing as he remembered. "When Rita twisted her ankle, you made it a game to see who could carry her the farthest, and so we weren't slowed down too much and kept having turns. And you have that story that you tell yourself as you're working. I wish I was more like that."

"Now you're joking," Twila mumbled, ducking her head. But even in the darkening twilight, Valiant could see the pleased smile crossing her lips. She rolled to her knees. "Your turn. What's one of your flaws that you want to change."

Valiant considered for a long moment, then, "I wish I didn't have to have everything so structured. I wish I could be more flexible."

"You plan things out and never have to stop to worry about what comes next. That makes you more efficient," Twila responded at once. "I admire that about you. It's one thing that I know I'd benefit from if we stay matched."

His heart picked up pace, and Valiant couldn't keep the note of hope from his voice as he asked, "Then you're going to consider it?"

"Yeah. I feel like we might actually have a shot at making this work... I don't want to give up on the possibility of being friends," Twila said. She flopped back to the ground and pointed at the sky. "Besides, I don't want to upset the stars. They're rooting for us, and who am I to say they're wrong?"

ELEVEN

"There was a marked change after that," Twila remembered. "I'm not sure if it was because we were both more comfortable with each other or just because that's the way it always would have been if we had allowed ourselves a shred of vulnerability with one another. Anyway, neither of us did much with the strongbox for a few days, and when Valiant got word his grandmother had had a turn for the better, he invited me to meet his family."

The field stretched as far as the eye could see, green and golden brown. Twila knelt back, stretching. Though she wore a straw hat, the sun was beating down on her, and she was certain she had sunburned already.

"I didn't realize that there was so much work involved in farming," she said to Valiant, who had come back to help her weed her row. Everyone else in his family was quite a way down the field, working quickly.

"There's always work to do on a farm; it's why you find so many farming communities where we work together," Valiant replied.

Twila nodded and bent back over her work. It was certainly repetitious and dull. Valiant's grandmother sat ahead of the weeders, reading aloud from a book, but Twila had fallen so far behind that she couldn't hear the story anymore.

"I get why you said you couldn't take vacations in summer, though," she said as she shuffled along, careful to pull out the choking weeds while leaving the small carrots behind. "With the never-ending work here... I hope your family isn't suffering because you've had to stay at the Institute."

Valiant let out a heavy breath. "Well... no, they haven't. Not really. I mean, we are a community, and there are plenty of workers. In the end, we have enough so that one missing person doesn't make or break the harvest."

"But one more set of hands makes it a little lighter for everyone else?" Twila offered.

"Yeah, there is that," Valiant admitted.

Twila studied him. Why wasn't he willing to say that even if his family didn't truly suffer, his absence still made a difference, not only for them but his entire community? It had to make a difference for him as well.

Was it because he was trying to spare her feelings? Since it was partly her fault, he wasn't here with his family the entire summer.

"It sure gives you time to think," she said, not voicing her concerns. They finally reached one another and cleaned up the last of the tiny weeds around the carrots. Twila stood, stretching her back, and tipped up her hat to look at the sky. "It's got to be getting close to one."

"Yup. We'll have lunch here soon and take the afternoon off. It gets too hot to work all day." Valiant started up the row with Twila following him.

"You must really like to farm," she mentioned. "You wake up so early for it."

Valiant shrugged. "It's better to work when it's cool. But don't get too comfortable just yet; it's the first day. Normally, I end up sleeping all afternoon from after lunch to just before supper; then I'm awake all night."

"Oh. Oh, that makes sense why you're always skulking around the common room so late at night, then," Twila pondered, bobbing her head. They caught up to the rest of the group, and she had to lower her voice to avoid interrupting the story. "You're a night owl."

Valiant chuckled, and he leaned in to whisper. "You have no idea."

Her stomach fluttered. Twila bit her lip and concentrated on her work. She didn't want to think about fluttering feelings right now.

After lunch, they went to the river to cool down. It was beautiful, half a kilometer wide, with sandy slopes on either side that slowly disappeared into the tree line. A series of large rocks sat in the middle of the river, and Twila was surprised to find that it was both sluggish and crystal clear. At its deepest part, she could shift into her dragon form and barely touch the bottom.

She amused the local children by diving in as a human and popping up as a dragon to shoot streams of water at them, always careful to arc it enough to that they wouldn't be harmed. Valiant splashed around a little at first but soon found a place in the shade where he napped.

When she was done playing, Twila crawled over to join him, laying on her stomach to read. The sun was warm against her back, despite the shade, and it made her sleepy.

"Psst. Valiant," she whispered.

"Hmmm?" His eyes remained closed.

"Are you sleeping?"

Valiant rolled slightly, so his face was turned toward her. "Trying to. What's up?"

"Well. Not much. I just wanted to say I get it now. Why you're so close to your family."

Valiant's eyes opened. It appeared he was having a hard time adjusting to being awake because it took him a few minutes before he sat up. "What do you mean, *now* you get it?"

"I didn't understand before, but now I do. You're all so close, and this community just always pulls together. It's nice." Twila dug her hand into the sand and let the warm, dry grains filter through her fingers.

"You're not close to your family? Your parents?" Valiant pressed, awake now and interested.

Twila hesitated. Just like she hadn't been able to understand how tightly knit a family could be, she wasn't sure Valiant could understand how loose one could be. "No. Not close at all. Not this way, at least. I know if I have trouble, I can ask them for help, but they aren't really in my life all that much."

Valiant stared at her.

"I knew you wouldn't understand."

"I don't. What happened? Are they...?" He floundered for his words and lifted both his hands as though asking, *What?*

Twila rolled into a sitting position. "I was raised by my grandmother. My parents were too young to take care of me properly, I guess. They tried to make it all work, but when I was five, they realized it wasn't working. Grandma got custody of me, and my parents parted ways."

"They abandoned you?" Valiant sounded horrified.

"They gave up the idea that they could make it work, and they made sure that I was properly cared for and then left. They both visited a few times every year, but... they never felt like 'mom' and 'dad' to me." Twila dug her toes into the sand. "Grandma was the only family I really needed. Or at least, I thought so."

Valiant shifted closer to her and put an arm around her shoulder. "And that was one thing you wanted from your fated mate, wasn't it? A sense of family."

"Maybe," Twila murmured, digging her foot deeper into the sand.

His arms wrapped around her. Valiant pulled her into his chest, hugging her tightly. Twila stiffened at first at the unexpected, unfamiliar contact. Hugs weren't exactly her forte. Her grandmother loved her, but she always had a certain level of touch-aversion that meant they didn't hug very often.

But it felt, so food to be held like this. Twila relaxed against him, letting her head come to rest on his shoulder.

It felt... *safe* to be comforted like this. It occurred to Twila that despite five years at the Institute with the same classmates and friends year after year, she had never revealed this much about herself before.

Weird. It didn't seem like such a big deal for people to know. She wasn't the only baby born to teenage parents who had tried to take on the adult responsibility, only to find they weren't up to the task of raising a baby.

So why did it feel so monumental that she had told Valiant?

"I'm sorry," he whispered. "I'm sorry I wasn't the family you needed me to be. But I will be, Twila. Nothing else really matters... I'll be your family, and I'll always be here for you."

A lump swelled in her throat, and her eyes burned. She buried her face into his shoulder and clung to him, fighting the emotion that longed to break free.

CHAPTER

TWELVE

H erja kicked her feet in the air. "So, it's your fault I have to work in a garden for a million hours every week?"

Valiant and Twila glanced at each other. The story was taking longer than expected... best to hurry it up a bit. Valiant cleared his throat. "Well, we spent some time with my family and then came back to the Institute. From there, we figured out the final puzzle. The strongbox led us to the hollow of a tree, and inside we found the treasure."

Valiant fastened the necklace around Twila's neck. The emerald sparkled in a gold setting, far too modern to be an antique work, but it highlighted her beauty well. The 'treasure' also included a set of emerald cufflinks and a matching pair of pocket watches.

It became obviously clear that the headmasters set the whole thing up. Apparently, the only thing they thought could bring their wayward wards onto the same page was to tempt them with puzzles and riddles.

"I'm not sure whether I should be insulted or amused," Valiant said as he turned his new pocket watch over in his hand. It was a beautiful bronze piece that told the time in twenty-four hours rather than twelve, just the way he liked.

Twila checked her reflection in the mirror and hummed. "I'm going with begrudgingly grateful while also being peevishly annoyed."

"Poetic," Valiant chuckled.

Twila turned to him with a cheeky smile. "I figured it out when we found the strongbox in the pond. No way could so many students go swimming there without finding it."

Valiant couldn't help but chuckle. "The pond is actually a fairly recent addition to the grounds."

"Ah. So, we each used our own knowledge and intuition to figure out the truth." Twila swished this way and that as she admired her new necklace. "This will go nicely with that forest-green romper of mine, won't it? The one with the lace sleeves."

"Oh, I remember that one. You wore it to the second-year matching Ceremony this year, didn't you?" Valiant asked, as though the image of Twila with her dark hair all in cascades of curl and ribbon and that velvet suit draped over her elegant form wasn't burned into his mind.

Yeah. But of course, I only noticed her because I didn't like her, he thought, sarcastic with himself. How had he managed to lie to himself so thoroughly for so long?

Twila turned back to him and leaned against a chair. "And you were wearing those dark blue robes. You looked like a magnificent king-priest of old. I remember because I kept dreaming of you in those robes for, like, a week after."

Heat flooded his cheeks even as a goofy smile spread over his face. "Oh, really? So, you liked the way I looked?"

"Oh, I was only dreaming of you because I was so utterly disappointed I hadn't gotten a proper fated mate," Twila drawled, an overly serious expression on her face while also more than a hint of sardonic self-depreciation in her voice.

"At least now we know, right?" Valiant asked. "Regardless of who set this up and why... I can't thank them enough that we can be friends now."

Twila nodded. "Yeah. We have that... I'm glad we figured out how to start to work with our bond rather than fighting it." Her shoulders slumped as she slowly sank into the chair. "I can't promise I'll always be reasonable or communicate the way I should. I can't promise I'll always be a suitable mate... but I'll try."

Valiant took in her words, surprised at how serious she was about this.

"Why are you telling me this?" he asked, head cocked to one side.

Twila looked away and shrugged.

Valiant studied her for a moment longer before he handed over her pocket watch. "All right, let me ask you something else. Do you expect me to be a perfect mate?"

Twila scoffed.

"I'll take that as a no."

"Oh! I didn't mean... I meant, of course, I don't expect you to be *perfect*. I didn't—" Twila shut her mouth quickly and shook her head, clearly embarrassed.

Valiant stuck his tongue out at her teasingly. As he hoped, it made her smile. She rolled her eyes at him and stuck her tongue out, too.

"No, I don't expect you to be perfect. Nobody's perfect," Twila said.

Aha! There it was. Exactly what Valiant wanted her to stay. "And you're somebody. You're not nobody, so why would you expect me to think you're going to be perfect? If we can go for three years fighting over everything only to turn it around in one summer, I'm pretty sure I don't expect perfection from you."

"That's not the same."

"So, you only expect perfection from yourself, then?"

Twila narrowed her eyes at him. "What are you getting at?"

"What I'm getting at is that you should extend the same grace to yourself as you extend to me. That is, as long as you know, I'll try my best, too." Valiant spread his hands, shrugging. He wasn't entirely certain what he was saying anymore. "I guess what I mean is, we do seem to complement each other's strengths and weaknesses, and as long as we both cover for each other and we try to make it work... we have a chance?"

"You have a point." Twila stroked her necklace as she leaned back in her chair. "So. Now that we've found the treasure and the headmasters can giggle to each other about finally getting us to get along, what will we do to get back at them?"

Valiant's heart dropped. "Wait, what?"

"We can't just let them get away with tricking us like this."

"What happened to the serious conversation we were just having?"

"We were done it, weren't we?"

Valiant threw his hands into the air. "Oh, I'm going to have to get used to this whiplash you put me through, aren't I? We're still talking about one thing, and your mind has skipped another five topics, and suddenly you've got a full battle plan in place."

"No, not a full battle plan," Twila protested. "I don't know how we'll get the itching powder into their underwear. Breaking into their room seems like it'd be a bit too far, and if we sabotaged the laundry, it could catch innocent parties in the crossfire."

She couldn't be serious. Could she?

"We could also toilet paper their carriage, but they don't really go anywhere, so chances are it'll get cleaned up before it affects them." Twila tapped her chin. "I'm thinking an epic showdown. We go to the dining hall and, in the middle of dinner, start screaming at each other until you challenge me to a duel and—"

"What are you talking about?" Valiant exclaimed. "No! I'm not going to do any of that!"

Twila's eyes sparkled. "No?"

"No! That's... that's... you can't do that."

"What about if you distracted them and I tied their shoelaces together?"

Valiant narrowed his eyes suspiciously at her. Twila smiled sweetly in return. It occurred to him suddenly that this wasn't the first time she had done something like this. Could it be that she was uncomfortable with the weight of their conversation, and she switched it like this, so she could pretend like nothing was wrong?

And as he was sitting there, mulling over this potential revelation, something else occurred to him.

Summer was ending.

It had flown by, and they were coming to the beginning of the harvest season. Soon, the students would start returning. The new first-years would come and take over the dorms that had been theirs for the last five years.

In only a few weeks, everything would change. And Valiant had no plans, no idea of what he was going to do afterward. He didn't even know how to make plans. It was terrifying. His entire future was set before him, and for the first time, he didn't know what he was going to do with it.

Up until now, it had only been his future. But now he had a mate. He and Twila had accepted their match, and they would continue to learn and grow together. So, what did that mean? Where would it take them?"

"Valiant?" Twila asked, a furrow forming between her eyebrows.

"Cake," he blurted.

Twila looked at him strangely.

"We'll make a cake and fill it with raspberry jam. But we decorate it like a fish or something. Then, when they cut into it, it looks gross. Or something."'

Twila laughed. "Let's do it!"

CHAPTER

THIRTEEN

"For as long as I thought the summer would be, it ended up being over so fast," Twila said, leaning back into the swinging bench. "Once Valiant and I came to the decision that we were going to take romance off the table and become the best-fated friend-mates we possibly could, it was like I couldn't stop thinking about how handsome he was. It frustrated me to no end; I was terrified that these feelings cropping up would ruin our friendship before it was even established."

It was the night before Twila and Valiant would go through their test once more to see whether they could actually graduate after the summer. And she couldn't sleep.

Twila had never worried about tests. She always figured that she had studied enough and would pass or hadn't studied enough and she'd have to try harder next time. Grades were never super important to her; it was about the learning.

Tonight, though, all she could think of was the consequences if they didn't perform to the headmasters' satisfaction. Even though she and Valiant were getting along now, even though they had decided to learn how to be mates, what if the headmasters decided they'd be better off without mates at all?

She tossed, turned, and nearly fell off her bed. At that point, Twila knew there was no further point in just lying awake with her thoughts. She got up and pulled on a jacket over her pajamas and stuffed her feet into her boots.

The night was clear and oddly cold for this time of the year. Twila breathed in deeply, letting her feet take her along the familiar pathways. It seemed so impossible that this could be her last chance to walk along this path... or it could be the start of yet another semester full of walking through it.

The Institute had become her home. After her grandmother passed, the house was given to her, but Twila had seen no point in keeping it. It was a big house, far too big for one person, so she had arranged the sale to the village. It was now used as a hospital.

It was only hitting Twila now that she didn't have anywhere that was *hers* to go to. Visiting Valiant's family only drove that fact in deeper.

A sigh whistled from her lungs as she lowered her gaze back to the path... only to see a figure shrouded in the night, standing on a nearby hill as he gazed toward the sky. Valiant. Twila didn't have to see his face to know it was him.

She padded over to him and silently stepped up to his shoulder, turning her face to gaze at the stars.

"Can't sleep?" Valiant asked.

"No."

"Me, neither. I thought I'd come out and look at the stars a bit. I've always loved nighttime."

Twila wrapped her arms around herself. She preferred dawns and mornings to wake up after a deep night's sleep and to tackle everything the day presented. As she stood there with Valiant, though, she felt a softness to the world. A sense of quiet, of peace.

"You see those three stars in a row, with the two above them?" Valiant asked, pointing.

Twila searched the area of sky he gestured to. "No. I see a lot of stars."

"Here." He pulled a paper and pencil from his pocket and jotted down five points. "This formation."

Once she knew what to look for, Twila found them quickly.

"That's known as the first dragon," Valiant explained. "The story goes that when the Sun blessed the land with dragons, the first to be turned eventually was mortally wounded by a giant bear that was terrorizing a village of the First Ones. The people wept at the loss, and the stars, moved by their tears, brought the dragon's soul to be a guide at night."

Twila leaned into him. "That's somehow both beautiful and tragic."

"Most stories of the stars are," Valiant admitted. "Our past is full of legends of pain and suffering. I think it reminds us to be grateful and to protect those who don't have the same good life as we do."

"Is there a 'first witch' up there, too?"

Valiant drew some more dots on the paper, then showed Twila how to follow the lines made by the first dragon to find the first witch. "She was the dragon's mate, and after his death, she took up his good work. She healed and worked hard to bring life and freedom to the First Ones. Upon her death in old age, the stars reunited them. Now, they are always in harmony together. Doesn't matter what time of year it is; you can always see them together."

"That's just a little romantic, don't you think?"

"Yeah. I do." Valiant turned to her. "You want to travel. I'm bound to my home, at least to begin with. I don't expect you to orbit your life around mine."

Twila searched his gaze, but with only starlight to guide her eyes, she couldn't decipher him.

"Once we've completed tomorrow's test and we've graduated, I'll be heading home. I'm going to spend the harvest with my family and help get everything ready for the winter. I'll be spending the winter at home so my parents can still go visit my siblings without worrying about Grandma." Valiant slid his arm around her waist. "I don't want you to think you have to come with me."

"I don't like the idea of separating, though," Twila admitted quietly.

"I know. I don't, either. I just... I need to be with my family. After the winter, I don't know. I'll always have reasons and excuses to stay at the farm. I'm not ready to say this is my time to leave, though."

Twila contemplated the problem. She loved the idea of spending the winter with Valiant, but at the same time, these feelings were coming at her too hard and too strong. The expected romance was rearing its head, and she didn't know how to deal with it. All she knew was that she didn't want a romance yet.

"We can write to each other," she suggested.

Valiant nodded.

"If I stay with you, I'm afraid I'll want to be married and pregnant by the end of next year," she admitted in a rush. "And it terrifies me. I'm not ready to be in love. I'm not ready to have that sort of commitment, Valiant. I don't know myself well enough yet."

Valiant turned, putting his hands on her shoulders. "I'm not ready for that, either. Even though right now, I'd like nothing more than to kiss you, it's not the right time," he whispered.

"We barely know each other," Twila whispered back.

"One summer where we stopped fighting isn't enough to jump into anything more," Valiant agreed, pulling his head out of the clouds. "Especially if there's any possibility for children. You're very right about that. I don't know myself well enough, either. I want to learn more about myself."

"And not just in the highly structured life at the Institute," Twila said.

"Exactly."

"And we still need to get to know each other again, too. Make sure that we really have learned how to stop fighting all the time."

Valiant nodded, silently agreeing with her. As they stood there, connected only by the lightest of touches, Twila felt something stirring in her. Whether it was the bond between them or a newfound sense of purpose, she wasn't sure.

But the future had never seemed more exciting. She would figure herself out. She'd try out different jobs and different tasks, and when she returned, she would know herself better.

And she'd write to Valiant. She would let him get to know her, the real her she was too afraid to share with anyone else. In doing so, she would get to know him. They would learn and grow together, and they'd figure out what being fated mates meant to them.

Valiant brushed a lock of hair from her forehead. "We should go back inside. We've got a big day tomorrow."

"Yeah, we do." Twila stepped back, breaking the physical connection between them. Though she instantly mourned that loss, she knew it was the right choice.

They needed time. And time they would have. Who knew... one day, they might just be the stuff that stars are made of.

FOURTEEN

Valiant took Twila's hand in his and brought it to his lips. "I stayed with the farm for another year, working with my family before I decided to pursue further education. Twila and I wrote letters back and forth, but we didn't see each other again until I started my training to be a teacher."

"So let me get this straight," Herja said slowly. "You started off your relationship as fated mates hating each other. Then once you started to not hate each other, you just stopped spending time with one another?"

Twila laughed. "I know it must seem impossibly old for you, but nineteen is very young. At least, it was for me. The best course of action for both of us was taking a unique approach to our relationship. And we came out stronger for it. We got married eventually and had three beautiful children."

Valiant stared, the bench swaying back and forth again, sighing in satisfaction as he looked up at the stars. "So, the point is, it's not a simple matter of liking or disliking your mate. It's not even a matter of romantic attraction. More often than not, mates do end up together romantically, but it must be a choice you make."

"The most important thing about having a mate is working together. You'll have to figure out what the best course is for the two of you and stick with it." Twila patted Herja's hand. "There's nothing wrong with wanting romance, of course. Just make sure you want it, rather than expecting it because it's expected."

Herja slid off the bench and stretched her back. "I guess that makes sense. But I don't really understand one thing. If it's not about liking or disliking your mate, how come it took until you stopped disliking each other for you to start to work together?"

Twila shook her head. "You have that backward. We only stopped disliking each other because we worked together."

"There is a grand thrill to falling in love," Valiant added. "But relationships cannot be forced. Neither can they be neglected. My advice to you is to communicate openly with all the witches of your year and work with them. Try not to decide who your mate is before the ceremony, as tempting as it is."

Something flashed over Herja's expression. Embarrassment, maybe. Guilt? Valiant bit back a smile. Knowing her, she had already decided who would logically be her mate. Ah, well. Children were apt to do such things.

"Thank you for telling me your story," Herja said as she gathered up her book bag. "It's given me a lot to think about."

She gave both headmasters a hug, and they wished her a good night. Herja skipped off, her bookbag tucked tight under her arm. Twila pushed off the ground a little harder than she had before, sending them swaying faster.

"I worry about her. She's so much like me at that age."

"Why worry, then? Look how you turned out... I'm sure she'll have just as satisfying a career," Valiant replied. He nuzzled against his wife's neck, stealing a few kisses on her throat.

Twila bent her head as she giggled. "Ooh, look at us. A couple of old lovebirds still necking on the love swing."

Valiant pulled away. "Now that just sounds dirty."

"Not as dirty as—"

"No," Valiant said, holding up a hand. "Not when the children might see."

Twila gave him the same impish smile she'd been giving him for the last few decades. Then she settled into his arms, still giggling to herself. Valiant knew her well enough to know she was going to unleash a barrage of dirty jokes on him as soon as they were in their private chambers for the night.

Some things never change. Not that he'd want them to.

As they swung idly back and forth, Valiant thought of all the years between then and now. It hadn't been an easy road. They had both made serious mistakes over the years, some worse than others, and it had taken a lot of communication and forgiveness to heal.

He wouldn't trade it for anything. Even the worst times were worth it because he had his perfect match at his side throughout it all.

"You're beautiful. You know that, right?" Valiant asked her.

"Oh, you flatter me." Twila fluffed her grey hair. It had grown coarser as it lost its color, but that gesture never failed to drive him crazy.

Valiant wrapped his arms around her, pulling her tightly into his embrace, and kissed her deeply. Twila sighed as she combed her fingers through his hair, now white more than silver. Their kisses might not have the fiery passion they once had, but there was passion aplenty all the same. Each touch of their lips had a thousand memories behind it, and none of it would have been possible if not for a simple treasure hunt.

Treasure hunt.

He reluctantly broke their kiss. Twila followed his lips as he pulled back.

"Hmmm, you look like you're thinking," she said as she pecked him on the cheek.

"I am. You said we should stimulate the students' minds more than the usual fare?" Valiant grinned as he already started planning some truly awful poetry to confuse them. "Let's create a treasure hunt. We can have them running all over the campus and trying to figure out the clues."

Twila's eyes lit up. "That's perfect! And we can have a couple of false ends, with a handful of trinkets that are a letdown before they get to the ultimate prize. I'm thinking something big. Like a... horse."

"A horse?"

"It's the biggest thing I could think of." Twila shrugged. "We can figure that out later. The main thing is how we are going to approach it. Will the students know that we're behind it, or should we play it like we're looking for the treasure, too?"

Valiant drummed his fingers against his knee. "Herja will know instantly we're behind it. Let's say that it's something that we put together when we were students here and only just remembered or something like that."

Herja would still see through it; perhaps most of the students would. But it was more fun to think of the treasure being hidden here for years and years rather than just randomly stuck somewhere recently.

As they sat, with the stars twinkling above them and a sea of memories behind them, Valiant had never felt more content. He loved this place, this home that they'd built at the Institute.

"We should head inside," Twila said eventually. "I don't want your back to get any worse."

"My back will be fine. I want to watch the stars a while longer."

And so, they stayed, arms wrapped around each other, and watched as the stars slowly changed position over them. Valiant counted each one and thanked it for knowing who his perfect match was, even when he himself didn't know.

EARLY THE NEXT MORNING, Twila lay in bed, watching Valiant sleep. It had become her custom over the many, many years that they were married. He was still a night owl, and she was an early bird. His chest rose and fell as he slept, and her gaze traced over each familiar wrinkle and line in his face.

Oh, he was so handsome. He is as much of a looker now as he was fifty-plus years ago. The loving father of her children. Her perfect match.

The stars certainly knew what they were doing when they paired her with him. The happiness he had given her was more than she had ever expected. She slipped out of bed quietly and got dressed for the day.

There was still a lot to do at the Institute... such as setting up a new treasure hunt.

Did you enjoy Twila and Valiant's story?
Please consider leaving a review on Goodreads, Bookbub or your favorite retailer. Reviews help me reach new readers.

Read **The Quest for the Sacred Tree**, the second book in the ***Defenders of the Realm series***!

Join my newsletter for writing updates, sneak peaks, review copies, sales, and giveaways!
www.mhlebeault.com

www.ingramcontent.com/pod-product-compliance
Lightning Source LLC
Chambersburg PA
CBHW050903120626
46554CB00003B/989